Disney's DuckTales

Down the Drain

Text by Justine Korman
Illustrated by Willy Ito and Darrell Baker

A GOLDEN BOOK • NEW YORK
Western Publishing Company, Inc., Racine, Wisconsin 53404

© 1990 The Walt Disney Company. All rights reserved. Printed in the U.S.A. No part of this book may be reproduced or copied in any form without written permission from the copyright owner. GOLDEN, GOLDEN & DESIGN, A GOLDEN LOOK-LOOK BOOK, GOLDENCRAFT, and A GOLDEN BOOK are trademarks of Western Publishing Company, Inc. Library of Congress Catalog Card Number: 88-81450 ISBN: 0-307-11726-X/ISBN: 0-307-61726-2 (lib. bdg.)
A B C D E F G H I J K L M

Scrooge McDuck scoffed at an article in the evening's *Duckburg Times*. "'Alligators seen swimming in storm drains under Duckburg!' That's the most ridiculous thing I ever heard," he declared.

"Quackeroonies!" exclaimed Huey, Dewey, and Louie as they gathered around Scrooge.

"Let's go on an alligator safari!" Huey suggested.

"Can I come, too?" asked Webbigail.

"No," said Dewey. "Nobody wants a girl along on a safari."

Louie agreed. "You'd only be in the way."

"Stop being silly!" Scrooge said. "There are no alligators in Duckburg."

"And you boys are not going anywhere tonight," began Scrooge's kindly housekeeper, Mrs. Beakley, "except to bed!"

Then Scrooge gasped and jumped right out of his chair.

"Take a gander at this!" he exclaimed, pointing a shaky finger at the *Times*.

Huey, Dewey, and Louie piled on top of one another to read the article:

CRIME WAVE HITS DUCKBURG

Duckburg police are puzzled as jewelry, rare coins, and other valuables keep disappearing from local stores. With no broken windows or unlocked doors, Duckburg's crime-stoppers can't understand how the crooks are getting in and out.

"I don't like the sound of that," said Scrooge nervously. "Not one bit!"

That night Scrooge tossed and turned in his bed as terrible visions swam before his eyes. He imagined his beloved billions gushing out of the giant money bin in a tidal wave of gold coins.

"There's nothing to do but check on the little darlings," Scrooge said as he hopped out of bed.

Huey, Dewey, and Louie weren't asleep, either. They
were busy packing for their alligator safari. Webbigail
watched and listened from behind the door.

"Shhh! It's Uncle Scrooge!" said Huey as he heard
Scrooge's footsteps.

"Where is he going?" Dewey wondered.

Louie shrugged. "We'd better follow him. You never
know what kind of trouble he'll get into without us Junior
Woodchucks looking out for him."

The nephews grabbed their safari gear and ran off to
follow Scrooge.

Scrooge went to his money bin and basked in its golden glow.

"A full bin is a happy bin!" he said with a sigh.

Then he heard the sound of a coin tumbling to the floor. Scrooge raced to his petty cash room. It was empty!

Suddenly Scrooge heard a muffled shuffling in the nearby room where he kept his money-cleaning machines.

Scrooge ran to the room and opened the door just in time to see an alligator slither down the drainage grate. The alligator was carrying a huge bag of gold.

"Stop, you thieving reptile!" Scrooge shouted as he grabbed its bumpy green tail. The alligator kept moving, pulling Scrooge down with it.

The alligator plunged into a flowing stream of water.
"An underground river!" Scrooge exclaimed.
Then he heard a roar as a powerful engine at the base
of the alligator's tail whirred to life.

"I didn't know these creatures had motors!" Scrooge said as he held on tight to the alligator's tail.

Suddenly Scrooge was water-skiing through the storm drains of Duckburg. His black stovepipe hat flew off his head into the churning water.

Huey, Dewey, and Louie had been following closely behind Uncle Scrooge. They gasped when they saw Scrooge's hat bobbing in the waves left by the speeding alligator.

Louie shined his flashlight at the *Junior Woodchuck Guide* so Huey and Dewey could read the directions for their inflatable raft. The nephews quickly inflated the raft, and soon they were paddling after Scrooge and the alligator.

Meanwhile, Webbigail, who had followed the boys, was left all alone by the underground river.

"Are you lost, miss?" asked a voice from the darkness.

Webbigail saw two river rats riding on a raft. The fat rat smiled, and the thin one looked down shyly.

"I'm Rocco," said the fat rat as he shook hands with Webbigail. "And this is my friend Ronald. Can we help you?"

Webbigail explained about Scrooge and the nephews taking off down the river. The rats agreed something strange was going on.

"All week we've been finding money, jewels, watches—all sorts of things!" said Rocco.

"If Uncle Scrooge and the boys are following crooks, they're going to need help," Webbigail said. "I've got to find them!"

"Hop aboard!" said Rocco. "Let's go!"

   As Webbigail and the rats took off after them, the
nephews were bouncing wildly up and down in their
rubber raft.
   Then all of a sudden angry alligators began attacking
the inflatable raft. With a bite from its mighty jaws, one of
the alligators ripped a hole in the raft.

Air hissed from the raft and suddenly sent it flying through the air. The boys landed on Scrooge, who lay sopping wet and breathless on a platform next to the underground river.

"Boys, what are you doing here?" Scrooge demanded.

"Where are we, anyway?" Huey wondered.

The nephews looked around. Above them was a bigger platform piled with all kinds of loot, including Scrooge's cash.

The nephews searched the *Junior Woodchuck Guide* for some clue to the mystery.

"Do alligators have motors in their tails?" Dewey asked.

"What I want to know is, do they like money?" Scrooge thundered.

The biggest alligator swam over to the platform and climbed up. As Scrooge and the nephews stared in disbelief the alligator's skin zipped off to reveal...

Big Time Beagle, leader of the notorious Beagle Boys.

"Tie them up, boys," Big Time ordered the other alligators, who were really Burger, Baggy, and Bouncer Beagle.

Big Time told his captive audience, "During our last prison break I noticed the storm drains that run all through Duckburg are connected to some very rich properties—like the Duckburg National Bank."

Scrooge winced. Whatever money he didn't keep in his money bin at home was in that bank.

"Come on," Big Time called to his gang after they finished tying up Scrooge and the nephews. "There won't be a line at the bank at this hour! And with Scrooge safely out of the way, we can empty the rest of his money bin, too. You can bank on that, McDuck!"

Then Big Time zipped himself back into his alligator suit, and he and the gang zoomed off.

After the Beagle Boys left, Scrooge wriggled and strained against the ropes, then gave up with a sigh.

"It's no use," Scrooge said. "We're doomed, and poor to boot."

"We're sorry we couldn't help, Uncle Scrooge," said Huey.

"I guess even the *Junior Woodchuck Guide* couldn't get us out of this jam," said Dewey.

"Hey, what's that?" asked Louie as they saw something approaching the platform.

Webbigail and the river rats paddled up to the platform.
"Webby, darling!" exclaimed Scrooge in amazement.
"You've saved us!"
"Quackeroonies! Are we glad to see you!" shouted
Huey, Dewey, and Louie.
Webbigail introduced Scrooge and the nephews to Rocco
and Ronald, who helped her untie the prisoners' ropes.

Then everyone piled onto the river rats' raft. They rode down to the police station, where Scrooge informed the police captain of the Beagle Boys' crimes.

The Duckburg Police Force arrived at the bank just in time to catch the Beagle Boys red-handed.

Duckburg's crime wave was finally over. Once again the Beagle Boys faced a long prison sentence. And happily for Scrooge, his petty cash room was once more filled to the brim.

The police captain gave Webbigail a medal for bravery. "Without your help, we might never have cracked this case," he said.

Webbigail beamed as Scrooge and the nephews looked on proudly.

Scrooge celebrated by taking a stroll with Webbigail through his money bin.

"Uncle Scrooge, are you sure there are no real alligators in Duckburg?" Webbigail asked.

"More certain than ever," Scrooge replied. "And if there were any alligators around, they'd be no match for a clever duck like you!"